Yummiest Love

Lisa McCourt

Illustrated by

Laura J. Bryant

Orchard Books • New York
An Imprint of Scholastic Inc.

To my own yummy ones and to the
fabulous Isabella Dispoto, with heaps of yummy love.
— L.M.

To Nicole, Joe, and Cy.
— L.B.

I love your sweet bear hugs
and crazy warm kisses
and the red crayon hearts
you draw just for me.

I love your wild belly laugh —
so delicious to my ears,
I'd do my silly face a hundred times
just to hear it again and again.

I love your scrumptious smell —
when you're soaped and rinsed
and squeaky clean,
and even when you're not.

I love the questions you ask —
so many questions
that one storybook
can take a whole afternoon of sharing.

THE

I love your never-ending surprises.

Like when you hate broccoli.

Then it's your favorite.

Then you hate it.

Then it's your favorite.

I love your free, courageous spirit,
even when it trips you up
and you need Band-Aids or kisses
or just the right words to help you find it again.

I love the snuddle we invented —
a cross between a snuggle and a cuddle,
but better and warmer than either of them.
Your snuddles are the best thing in my world.

I love the way you sing and dance
and tell me stories,
then dream up new songs
and dances and stories for me.

I love our gentle, quiet times.
And the warmth of your small body
and the beautiful beating
of your perfect little heart.

I treasure every memory we make.
Memories of special days
and all the days in between,
each day wrapped in the yummiest love.

I love all our tickles
and tumbles and smiles.
I love everything you've been
and everything you'll become.

It seems impossible that I could love you more each day
but that is what happens.
You keep changing and growing and that will never stop.
All I can do is hang on for the ride.

I love you more than sunshine.
More than the moon
and the million twinkling stars.
Thank you for being the you that you are.